W9-DAL-730

VESTAVIA HILLS
RICHARD M. SCRUSHY
PUBLIC LIBRARY

1112 Montgomery Highway
Vestavia Hills, Alabama 35216

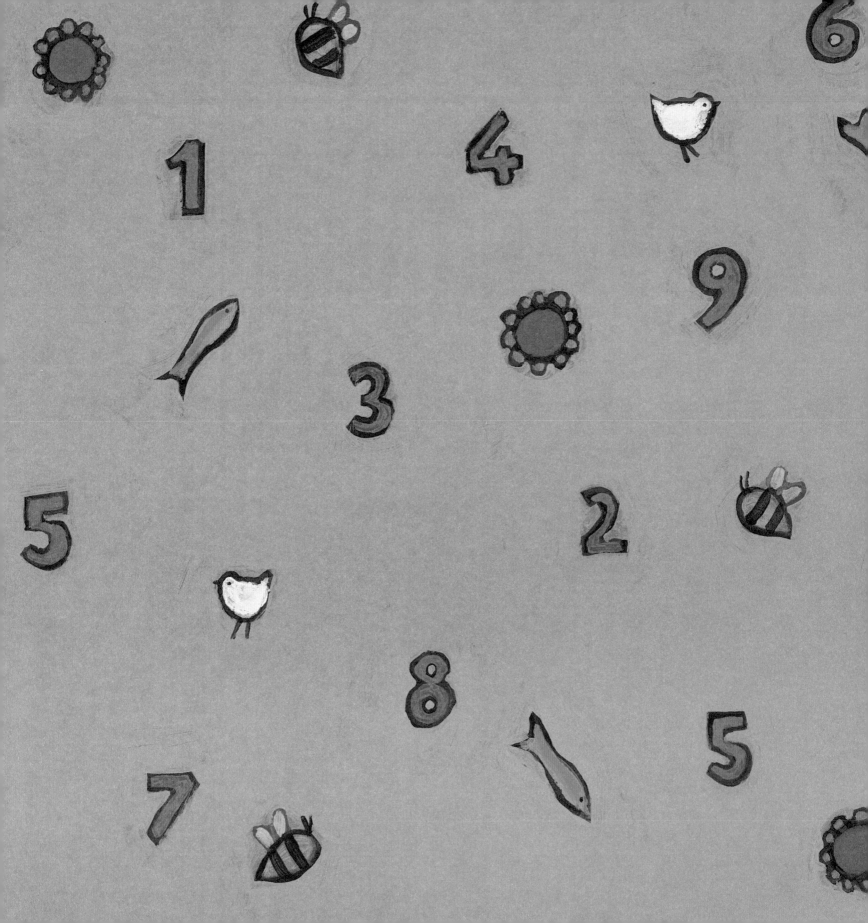

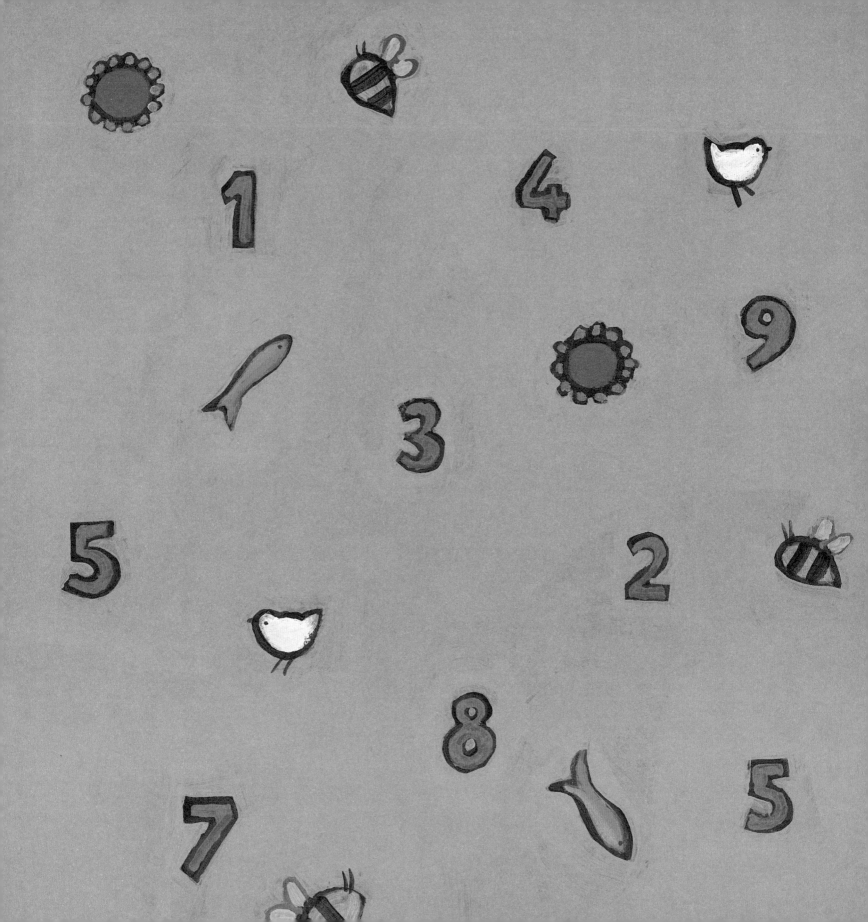

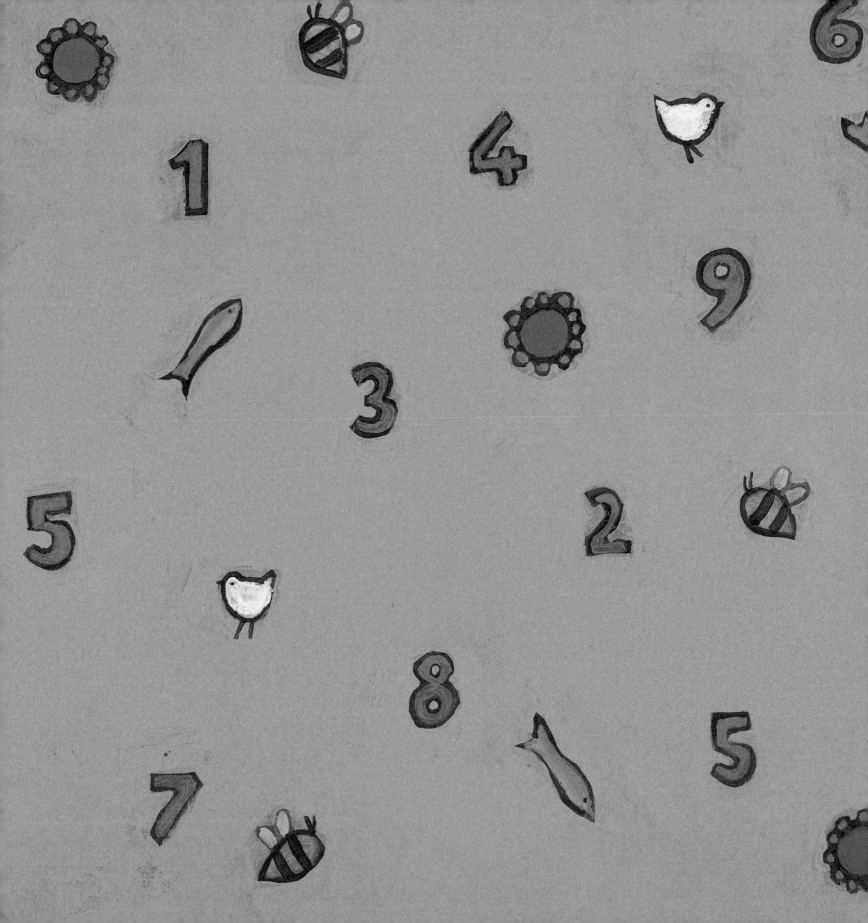

MAR 2 3 2004

CLEO'S COUNTING BOOK

Caroline Mockford

Barefoot Books

Celebrating Art and Story

VESTAVIA HILLS
RICHARD M SCRUSHY
PUBLIC LIBRARY

Let's count with Cleo
from one to ten.

Then let's count
back to one again.

6 7 8 9 10

One big gate.

2

Two small dogs.

Three singing birds.

Four
speckled
frogs.

5

Five
stepping
stones.

Six tall trees.

7

Seven flashing fishes.

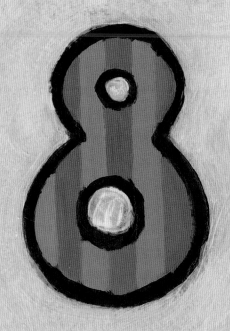

Eight
buzzing
bees.

Nine fluffy
chicks —
but where is
mother hen?

Here she comes
with one more
chick — and
that makes ten!

Cleo can count
from one to ten.

1 2 3 4 5

one
two
three
four
five

6 7 8 9 10

six eight ten
seven nine

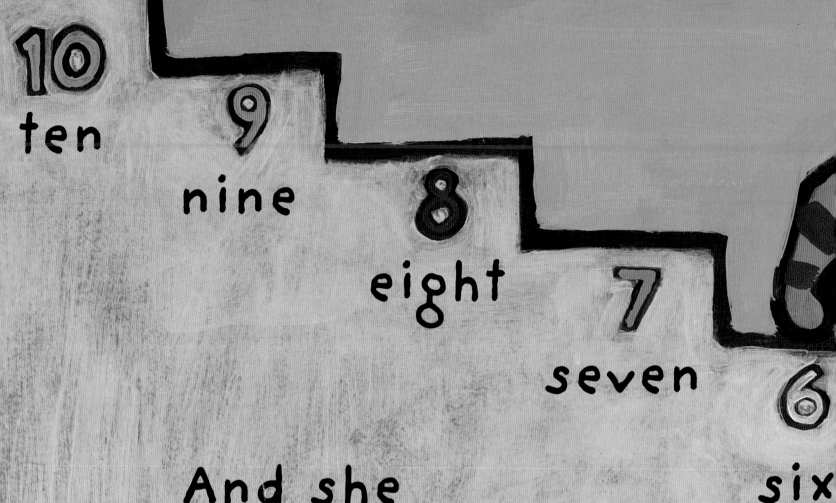

10 ten

9 nine

8 eight

7 seven

6 six

And she can count back to one again!

For Freddy and Felix — S. B.
For Phoebe and Hepzibah — C. M.

Barefoot Books
3 Bow Street, 3rd Floor
Cambridge, MA 02138

Text copyright © 2003 by Stella Blackstone
Illustrations copyright © 2003 by Caroline Mockford
The moral right of Stella Blackstone to be identified as the author and Caroline
Mockford to be identified as the illustrator of this work has been asserted

First published in the United States of America in 2003 by Barefoot Books, Inc.
All rights reserved. No part of this book may be reproduced in any form or by any means,
electronic or mechanical, including photocopying, recording or by any information storage
and retrieval system, without permission in writing from the publisher

This book has been printed on 100% acid-free paper
The illustrations were prepared in acrylics on 140lb watercolor paper
Design by Jennie Hoare, England
Typeset in 44pt Providence Sans Bold
Color separation by Bright Arts Graphics, Singapore
Printed and bound in Singapore by Tien Wah Press Pte Ltd

1 3 5 7 9 8 6 4 2

Publisher Cataloging-in-Publication Data   (U.S.)

Blackstone, Stella.
      Counting with Cleo / [Stella Blackstone] ; Caroline Mockford.
1st ed.
[24] p. : col. ill. ;   cm.   (Cleo the cat)
Summary: Cleo teaches kids to count from one to ten and back down to
one again, using all the objects and animals that she sees.
ISBN 1-84148-207-2
1. Cats — Fiction. 2. Counting — Fiction. I. Mockford, Caroline. II.
Title. III. Series.
      [E] 21   2003

Barefoot Books
Celebrating Art and Story

At Barefoot Books, we celebrate art and story with books that open the hearts and minds of children from all walks of life, inspiring them to read deeper, search further, and explore their own creative gifts. Taking our inspiration from many different cultures, we focus on themes that encourage independence of spirit, enthusiasm for learning, and acceptance of other traditions. Thoughtfully prepared by writers, artists, and storytellers from all over the world, our products combine the best of the present with the best of the past to educate our children as the caretakers of tomorrow.

www.barefootbooks.com

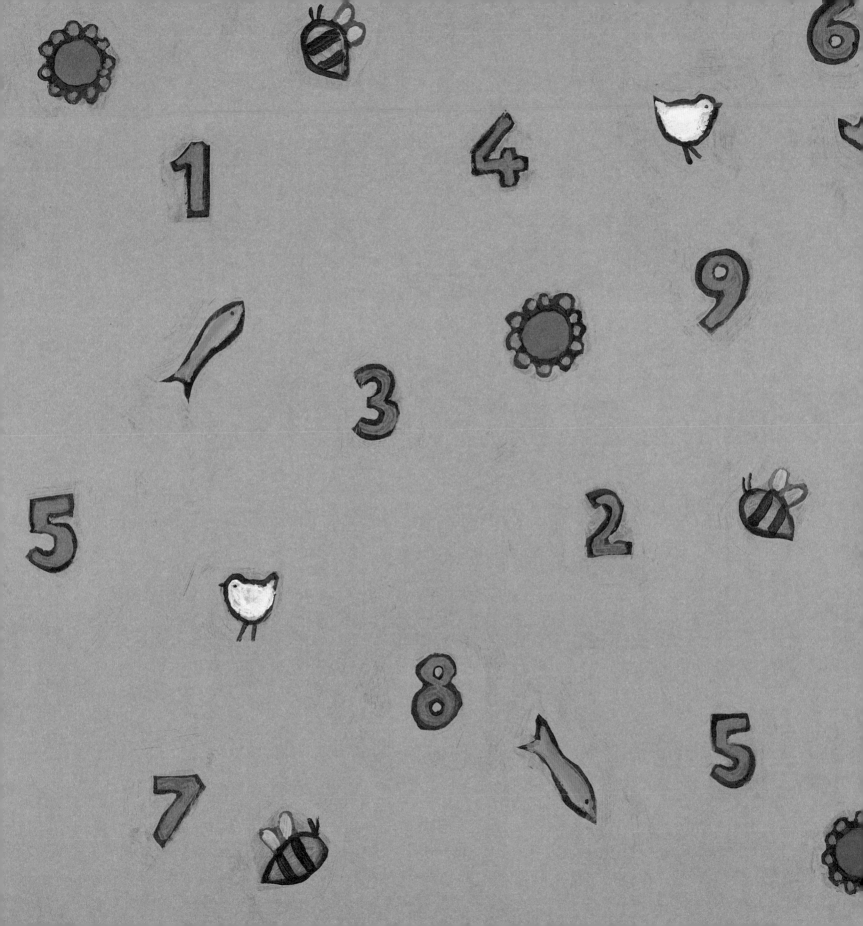